CAPTAIN FANTASTIC
I've GOT YOU

THIS BOOK BELONGS TO

....

THE
CAPTAIN FANTASTIC
COLLECTION

Published by Tommy Balaam, founder of Captain Fantastic

UK's number-one children's entertainment company

www.captain-fantastic.co.uk

Copyright © 2020 Tommy Balaam

Cover and illustrations by Daniel Howard, xxdanielhowardxx@gmail.com

Book design by Helen Nelson, www.jetthedog.co.uk

Editing by Ilsa Hawtin, www.wordsure.co.uk

ISBN: 9798649062473

CAPTAIN FANTASTIC

I've Got You

Tommy Balaam

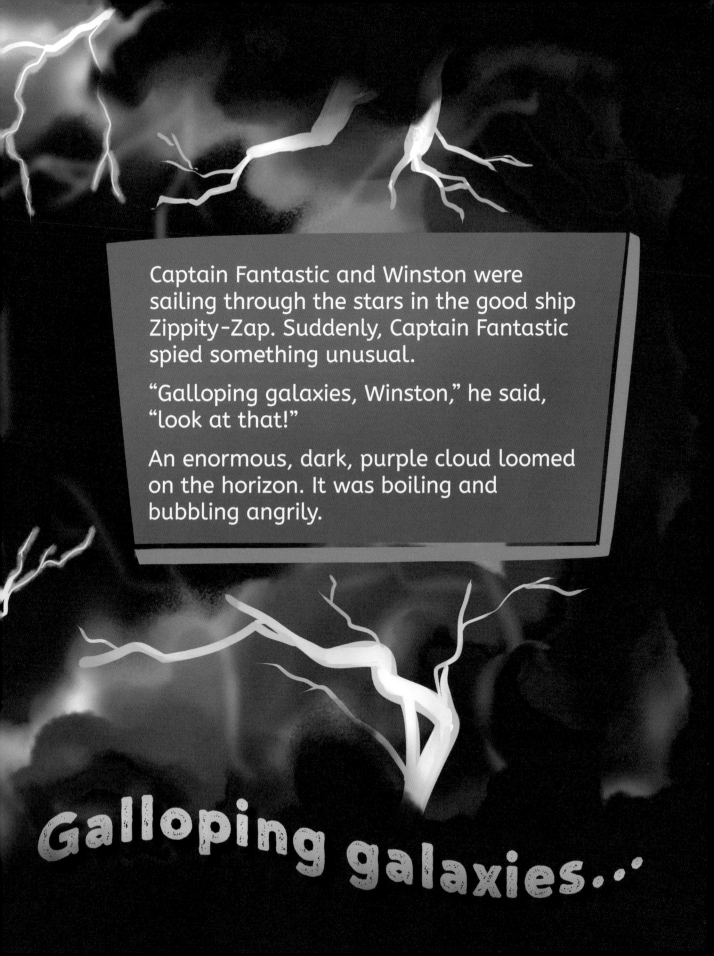

Captain Fantastic and Winston were sailing through the stars in the good ship Zippity-Zap. Suddenly, Captain Fantastic spied something unusual.

"Galloping galaxies, Winston," he said, "look at that!"

An enormous, dark, purple cloud loomed on the horizon. It was boiling and bubbling angrily.

Galloping galaxies...'

"Looks like we're in for some bad weather," said the captain, turning on the windscreen wipers.

Just then, the cabin grew dark and there was a great big enormous clap of thunder.

CLAAAAPBAAANG!

"Astronomical asteroids," said the captain. "A space storm, Winston!"

But Winston had disappeared.

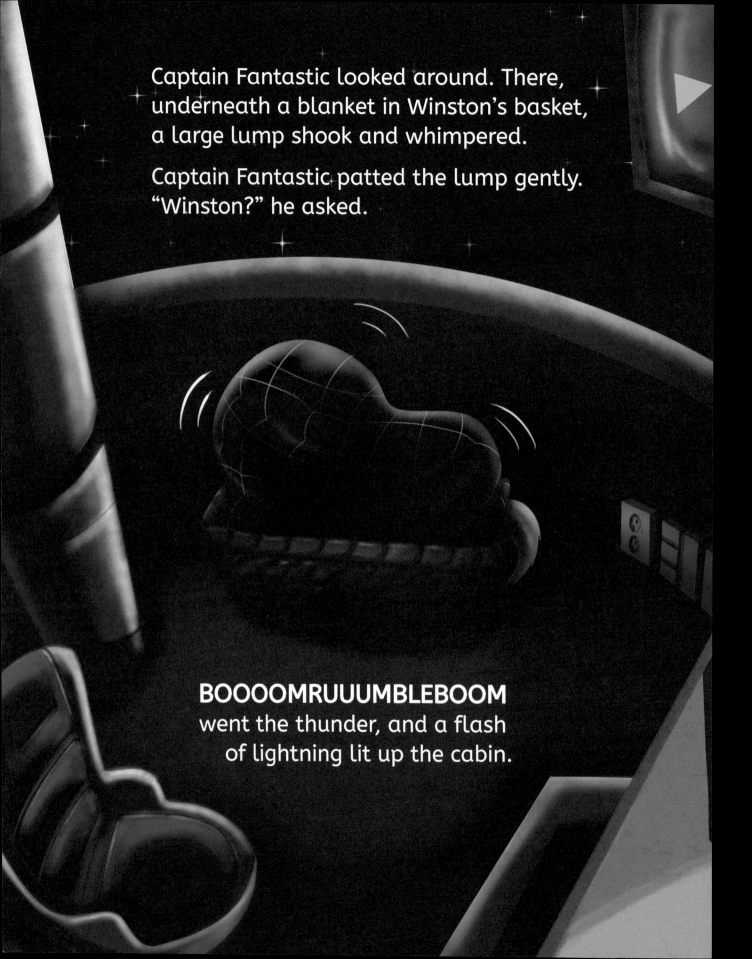

Captain Fantastic looked around. There, underneath a blanket in Winston's basket, a large lump shook and whimpered.

Captain Fantastic patted the lump gently. "Winston?" he asked.

BOOOOMRUUUMBLEBOOM
went the thunder, and a flash
of lightning lit up the cabin.

The lump gave a
frightened yelp
and shook harder.

"Oh, Winston," said the captain kindly, "it's all right! Don't be afraid – it's only a storm!"

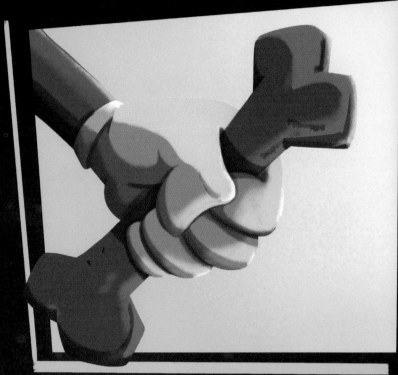

But Winston wouldn't come out.

The captain tried offering him a treat.

Then he tried putting on his favourite film.

He even tried telling jokes.

But it was no good.
Winston wouldn't budge.

Then Captain Fantastic had an idea.

"When I'm **really** frightened," he said to the sad, quivering lump, "there's only one thing that makes me feel better."

"In the dark and deepest black
When there's no hope of turning back
You're my light, shining through
I'm never alone, as I've got you."

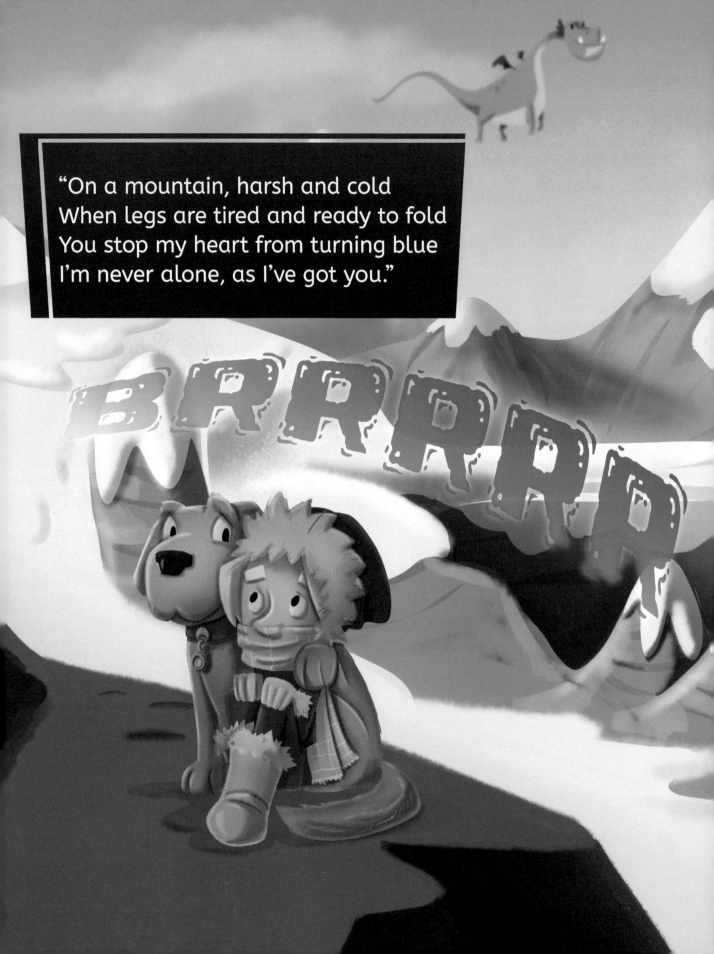

"On a mountain, harsh and cold
When legs are tired and ready to fold
You stop my heart from turning blue
I'm never alone, as I've got you."

"Stuck up to our waists in a dirty bog
With witches, bats, giants and frogs
You're brave, you're clever, loyal and true
I'm never alone, as I've got you."

SLOP!
SQUISH!
SQUELCH!

"Trapped undersea and gasping for air
Unable to escape the sea monster's lair
You've got the strength to pull us through
I'm never alone, as I've got you."

"Up the river without a canoe
Drifting fast without a clue
You always know just what to do
I'm never alone, as I've got you."

"But most of all, I need you to know
That no matter what the problem or woe
Please never worry of what may be
You're never alone, as you have me!"

Captain Fantastic gave the Winston-shaped lump a Great Big Enormous Hug.

The lump stopped shaking. Slowly, a soft, whiskery nose appeared. Winston peeped out.

"You mean it, Captain?" he asked, in a small, frightened voice.

"Of course!" said Captain Fantastic. "Even captains get scared, and where would I be without my Super Fantastic Space Dog?"

Winston jumped on Captain Fantastic and gave him a big, furry hug.

"Come on," said the captain, "let's have some hot cocoa."

Winston and the captain curled up together under the blanket and watched the lightning flash through the sky and across the stars.

The thunder rumbled and boomed, but Winston didn't mind.

"After all," he said to Captain Fantastic, "I've got you!"

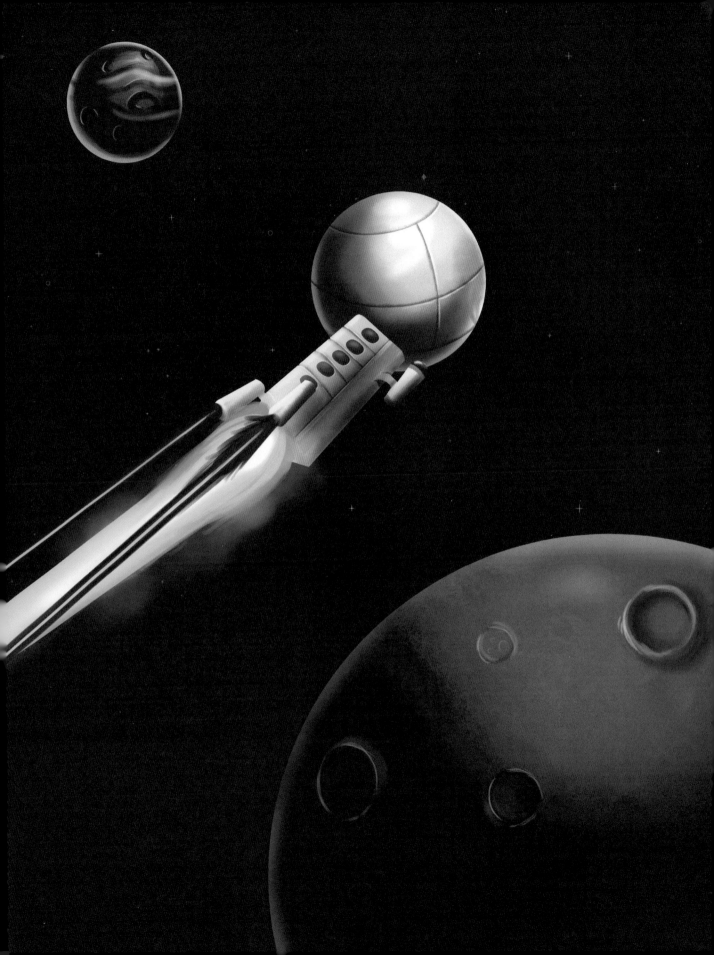

CAPTAIN
FANTASTIC

VOTED THE UK'S NUMBER ONE CHILDREN'S ENTERTAINMENT COMPANY

Look out for the next crazy adventure in this series: Chocolate Planet. Captain Fantastic and Winston are going to find themselves in a seriously sticky situation.

COME AND JOIN US!

Captain Fantastic offers hundreds of ways to entertain and educate children of all ages. We offer everything from virtual playdates to wellbeing courses, from books to merchandise … and (in our humble opinion) the best children's parties in the world!

Visit our website to find out more, and get in touch with any questions – we'd love to hear from you!

@CAPTAINFANTASTICKIDS

WWW.CAPTAIN-FANTASTIC.CO.UK

Printed in Poland
by Amazon Fulfillment
Poland Sp. z o.o., Wrocław

60670308R00021